BRAINTEAS[ERS]

From JEWISH FOLKLORE

Rosalind Charney Kaye

KAR-BEN COPIES, INC. ROCKVILLE, MD

In memory of my mother,
Bess Minuskin Charney,
who always loved a good puzzle.
—RCK

Library of Congress Cataloging-in-Publication Data

Kaye, Rosalind Charney.
Brainteasers from Jewish folklore / Rosalind Charney Kaye.
p. cm.
Summary: A collection of puzzling situations and stories from Jewish folklore, concerning outsmarting others, coping with those in power, and learning how to live.
ISBN 1-58013-001-1 (pbk.)
1. Jews—Folklore. [1. Jews—Folklore. 2. Folklore.]
I. Title.
PZ8.1.K175Br 1997
398.2'089924—dc21 97-2698
CIP
AC

Published by Kar-Ben Copies, Inc., Rockville, MD 1-800-452-7236
Printed in Mexico

CONTENTS

CLEVER PEOPLE/FOOLISH PEOPLE

COPING WITH NOBLEMEN

LESSONS IN LIVING

Animal Arithmetic

When an old woman died, her sons learned that she had left all her property to charity, except for her goats. Her oldest son was to inherit one half of her goats, the second son got one third, and the youngest son one ninth of the goats.

The problem was that there were 17 goats in all. Seventeen cannot be divided evenly into halves, thirds, or ninths. So the three brothers went to the rabbi and asked him for advice. How could they respect their mother's last wishes without the help of the village butcher?

After pondering the matter for a very long time, the rabbi brought over one of his own goats to help solve the problem. Did the goat know arithmetic better than the rabbi?

"My goat added to yours totals 18 goats," the rabbi explained. "Now you," he said to the oldest son "can take your half of the herd -- nine goats. And you," he said to the middle son, "can take one-third of 18 goats which is six goats. And you," he instructed the youngest son, "can take one-ninth or two goats. Nine plus six plus two equals 17 goats in all. There's one goat left, so I'll take my goat back."

Foresight

The rabbi stood up from his desk to stretch his legs. He walked once around the room, and when he sat down, his reading glasses were gone. Yet only ten minutes ago in that very room, he'd used them to read the Talmud. He hadn't left the room, and no one else had entered!

He looked carefully through his pockets, where he found several things he had accused his dear wife of losing. But he found no glasses.

Then he searched every drawer, box, and container large enough to hide a pair of reading glasses. Surely they had vanished!

The rabbi reached the only sensible conclusion. A dybbuk, an evil spirit, was tormenting him with magic.

Where were his reading glasses?

On top of his head, where he had pushed them when he rose from his books.

The Most Precious Thing

A rich man fell in love and got married. The couple lived happily, but they had no children. Believing that a marriage without children is not really a marriage, the husband followed an old custom and asked his wife for a divorce.

"It's no more my fault than yours that we haven't been blessed with children," she protested.

"I know that," he sighed. "And we have had a wonderful life together. Even so, you must leave and return to your parents' home. As my parting gift, you may take with you the most precious thing you can find in the house."

Their home was filled with beautiful dishes, silverware, candlesticks, samovars, blankets, and rugs, as well as fine clothing and jewelry. What did the wife choose to take with her?

She took her husband himself. He was so touched by her love that they stayed married. In less than a year they were blessed with a child.

King Solomon and the Queen of Sheba

King Solomon was known as the wise king, but the Queen of Sheba was not one to believe all she had heard. Arriving in Jerusalem with a magnificent caravan and many precious gifts, she decided to test Solomon's wisdom with some riddles.

"What water does not fall from the sky, or gush down from the mountains? It always comes from the same place, but sometimes it is sweet and sometimes it is bitter."

"What do you bury that isn't dead, and the longer it lies underground, the more alive it becomes?"

"What doesn't move anywhere when it is alive, but moves all over when it is dead?"

King Solomon guessed all the answers and made a very good impression. Can you do as well?

1. Tears 2. Seeds 3. Timber used to build a ship

The Lazy Artist

A king wished to build the most splendid palace imaginable. After years of construction, it was finally ready to be painted. Two artists were hired to make the palace look like no other in the world. The first artist was asked to decorate one side of each hallway, the second to adorn the facing walls.

The first artist searched the world for beautiful colors and designs, and spent five years painting wonderful images of animals and landscapes. The second artist spent most of his time doodling and daydreaming.

Finally the first artist was almost finished. The lazy artist began to worry, then to panic. With only a short time left to work, how could he equal the splendid pictures of his colleague?

He covered his walls with mirrors.

The Slow Ride

A king lay dying. He called his two sons to him and said, "As soon as the sun rises, mount your horses and ride to Jerusalem. The one whose horse reaches Jerusalem last will become the next king."

The two sons left as instructed. Each one rode as slowly as possible, trying to make sure he stayed behind the other. When Jerusalem was finally in sight, they both sat and rested, hoping the other would take off first. After what seemed like hours of sitting, each suddenly leaped onto a horse and galloped off as fast as he could. Why?

Each brother got on the other's horse.

The Best Way to Die

The Caliph of Baghdad planned to rid his palace of Jews, beginning with his own court jester.

"However," said the caliph to the clown, "since you amused me so much in the past, I will let you choose how you shall die."

The jester's answer allowed him to live for many more years. What was it?

The jester replied, "O wisest and kindest of caliphs, I choose to die of old age."

Cheating the Inquisitor

A murder in Spain had not been solved. This made the Grand Inquisitor look very bad, so he decided to accuse the Jews of the crime. As leader of the Jewish community, the rabbi was brought to stand trial.

"We'll leave the matter up to God," announced the inquisitor. "I'll put two pieces of paper in a box, one with the word GUILTY on it, one with the word INNOCENT. Whichever the rabbi picks will tell us the truth."

Of course the crafty inquisitor, knowing that no one would dare question him, wrote GUILTY on both pieces of paper! The rabbi suspected just a trick. What did he do to save himself?

The rabbi selected one paper, quickly stuffed it into his mouth, and swallowed it. Then he asked the inquisitor to read the paper that was still in the box. Naturally, it said GUILTY. "Then the one I ate must have said INNOCENT!" the rabbi exclaimed. And the much-astonished inquisitor had to let the rabbi go free.

The Little Sharpshooter

On his way home from military school, a young nobleman stopped to rest at an inn. Leaving his horse at the stable, he noticed a wall with a dozen bulls' eyes drawn in chalk. There was a bullet hole in the center of every one.

"How can this be?" he thought. The clean holes could only have been made by a rifle at a good distance. Even he himself, who had won his school riflery prize, could never have shot so well.

Questioning the villagers, he was astonished to learn that the sharpshooter was a small Jewish boy dressed in rags.

"But you're an insignificant little peasant," he told the boy.

"And I can barely lift a rifle, Your Excellency," the boy responded.

So how did the little boy manage to hit a bull's eye every time?

He shot first and then drew the target around the hole.

To Tell the Truth

Once an Arabian caliph issued a terrible order: “All Jews who come to my kingdom must identify themselves to the guards. If they lie, chop off their heads. If they tell the truth, hang them at once. And death to the guard who makes a mistake.” By this cruel law, the caliph planned to kill all the Jews of Arabia.

One day a Jewish woman arrived at the border. When the guards commanded her to identify herself, she said something that spared her life. What did she say?

She said, "I am a woman who is going to be beheaded today." By saying this, the woman made sure the guards would always make a mistake, thereby risking their own death. If they beheaded her, she would have been telling the truth -- and therefore should have been hanged and not beheaded. If the guards hanged her, she would have been telling a lie, and should have been beheaded.

What Was He Thinking

The famous philosopher, Rabbi Abraham ben Ezra, was captured by pirates and sold as a slave to a bishop. Soon after, the bishop was called before the king. If the bishop could answer the king's question, "What am I thinking?" he would be appointed the king's new minister. If he could not, he would have his head chopped off.

The bishop was frantic and confided in Rabbi Abraham. "Not to worry," said the rabbi. The next day, Rabbi Abraham dressed in the bishop's clothes and went to see the king. "So, your holiness," said the king to Rabbi Abraham, "what am I thinking?" Rabbi Abraham gave the correct answer. The bishop's head was saved, and Rabbi Abraham was rewarded with his freedom.

What did Rabbi Abraham say the king was thinking?

"You're thinking that I am the bishop."

One Hundred Rubles

The Czar of Russia learned the answer to a difficult riddle from a poor Jewish farmer working in his fields. He paid the farmer a ruble to keep the answer a secret.

"Swear," he said, "that you shall not breathe a word about it until you have seen my face again a hundred times."

The farmer took the ruble and promised. The czar then challenged his ministers to solve the riddle within 30 days.

The ministers all thought they were quite clever, but as the days passed, they began to get desperate. Then one of them remembered seeing the czar whispering with the old farmer. The minister had no trouble finding the farmer, but the farmer refused to tell him the answer.

"However," added the poor farmer, "if you are able to pay me 100 rubles, then I will tell you." The minister readily agreed.

When the czar learned that the answer to his riddle was the talk of the palace, he knew the old farmer had betrayed him. He had him arrested. The farmer was brought before him. "Your Czarness," he protested, "I did not break my promise."

How could the farmer have told the secret without breaking his promise?

The farmer had indeed seen the czar's face 100 times...stamped on each ruble the minister had paid him.

Why Did I Ask?

Mendel the shoemaker was working quietly at his cobbler's bench when who should burst in but the Emperor Napoleon! "Save me," the emperor screamed in panic. "They're going to kill me."

The good-hearted shoemaker hid Napoleon in his bed under a pile of old quilts, just as three enemy soldiers stormed into the room. They pierced their swords into everything, including the quilts on the bed, but found nothing and left.

Miraculously unharmed, Napoleon granted Mendel one wish as a reward for saving his life. Mendel was perplexed, since he was basically happy and had everything he needed. Finally, he asked Napoleon, "Tell me, if you don't mind, how you felt when the soldiers poked their swords into the quilts?"

Suddenly Napoleon turned red. He ordered his troops to tie the terrified shoemaker to a tree and shoot him.

"Ready!" The soldiers lifted their guns.

"Aim!" The soldiers aimed. Mendel said his last prayers.

But the emperor didn't say "Fire!" What did he say?

"Now you know how I felt!"

The Grateful Rabbi

Rabbi Akiba once went on a journey. He took along a donkey to ride, a rooster to wake him, and an oil lamp to light his way. After many hours of travel, he stopped by a village asking for a night's shelter. But the mean-spirited villagers turned him away and told him to sleep on the mountainside above the village.

During the night a lion ate his donkey, a wildcat ate his rooster, and a wind blew out his lamp. In the morning, he found that the villagers, too, had been visited by misfortune. Robbers had looted them in the middle of the night.

Rabbi Akiba praised God for his great blessings. He was thankful not to be in the village, or else he, too, would have been robbed. But what of the loss of his donkey, his rooster, and his lamp?

Rabbi Akiba believed that everything worked out for the best. Had the robbers seen the burning lamp, or heard the rooster crow or the donkey bray, they would have found and robbed him, too.

David and the Spider

Long before David was king, he came upon a spider in his garden.

"Lord," he said, "You have created many beautiful and wondrous things. But what good could a spider be to anyone? Surely you have made a mistake."

"There will be a time," God answered, "when this little mistake will be of great use to you."

And the time did indeed come. King Saul became fiercely jealous of David. He ordered his soldiers to follow David into the wilderness to kill him. David slipped into a cave just before Saul's soldiers came upon him.

As David crouched at the back of the cave, he watched a spider swiftly spin a web across the cave's entrance. This thin web was enough to keep the soldiers out, even with their knives and swords. How?

When the soldiers saw an unbroken web across the cave entrance, they assumed that no one had entered the cave in many days, and so they didn't search it. David's life was saved, and he understood that people depend on all God's creations.

Light Cargo

A terrible storm arose at sea. Fearing their ship would break apart unless they lightened the load, the passengers threw all their baggage overboard. Many were merchants who sacrified fortunes in rugs, furnishings, and silver. But even the poorest among them, a great Jewish scholar, tossed over his few possessions.

Mercifully, their boat was blown onto the shores of a foreign land. They were cast ashore with nothing but the clothes on their backs, and so had to beg for everything they needed. As the years passed the merchants continued to be needy beggars, but the poor scholar prospered. What was his secret?

Like everyone else, the scholar lost his worldly possessions at sea, but his true wealth was his knowledge, which weighed nothing and could never be lost.

Sources

All of the stories in this book were adapted from folktales appearing in English anthologies.

"The Best Way to Die," "Cheating the Inquisitor," "To Tell the Truth," "The Little Sharpshooter," "One Hundred Rubles," "Foresight," "Animal Arithmetic," and "Why Did I Ask?" from Ausubel, Nathan (ed.) *A Treasury of Jewish Folklore,* New York: Crown, 1975.

"What Was He Thinking" from an oral story from Morocco in Sadeh, Pinhas (ed.) *Jewish Folktales.* New York: Doubleday, 1989.

"The Most Precious Thing" from a story of the Midrash in Frankel, Ellen (ed.) *The Classic Tales: 4000 Years of Jewish Lore,* Northvale, NJ: Jason Aronson, Inc., 1989, and a Yiddish story in Ausubel.

"King Solomon and the Queen of Sheba" from stories of the Midrash in Ausubel and Frankel.

"The Lazy Artist" and "Light Cargo" from bin Gorion, Micha Joseph, *Mimekor Yisrael: Classic Jewish Folktales, Vol. III,* Bloomington: Indiana University Press, 1976.

"The Slow Ride" from an oral story in Sadeh.

"The Grateful Rabbi" from the Agada, appearing in Ausubel and in Frankel.

"David and the Spider" from Frankel.

"Light Cargo" from bin Gorion, and a story of the Midrash in Ausubel.

Several of the stories first appeared in *Shofar Magazine.*

ROSALIND CHARNEY KAYE holds a Ph.D in Educational Psychology from the University of Chicago and worked as a psychotherapist until the birth of her third child in 1986. She has studied art privately and at several schools in the Chicago area. To illustrate *Brainteasers from Jewish Folklore,* she developed a mixed media technique of collage and painting.